The Adventures of
BUZZ BEE
A Story about Epilepsy

Written & Illustrated by
Jacqueline Ann Gibson

ISBN-13: 978-1512022049

ISBN-10: 1512022047

This book is dedicated to Tony,
who is the best boy ever, and to
the memory of Dr. Fritz Dreifuss.

ACKNOWLEDGEMENTS

To Rosemary Merrell, J.J. Lendl, Flower, Bill, Trudy, Jack, Theresa, and all my friends who put up with me while I was writing this book.

Author's Note

10% of royalties from this book will
go to the Epilepsy Foundation to fund their
research.

It was the busiest time of the year in the hive. All of the bees were busy gathering nectar from the flowers before the winter.

Buzz Bee was working hard with all of the other bees. But unlike the other bees, Buzz Bee was worried and scared. Bad things were happening to him and he didn't know why. His brain was all mixed up and he didn't know what to do.

That particular day, he was on his way to check out a field that the other bees had told him about. They could make a lot of honey from all the nectar in the flowers there. Buzz Bee loved honey!

Suddenly, Buzz Bee found himself stuck smack dab in the middle of a flower.

"How did I get here?" cried Buzz Bee. "I can't believe this! I'm all mixed up again and now I can't even remember how to get out of here! What on earth is wrong with me?"

The next day, Buzz Bee, Buddy Bee, and the other bees were heading back to the field. All of a sudden, Buzz Bee started flying upside down.

"Oh, Buzz Bee! Stop playing around. Straighten up and fly right!" said Buddy Bee.

But Buzz Bee did not answer.

"What is wrong with him?" asked the other bees.

"I don't know what's happening," said Buddy Bee. "He told me he flew into the petals of a flower yesterday and couldn't get out. I wonder if something is wrong."

"Will he be all right?" asked the bees.

"He seemed all right after what happened with the petals yesterday. Maybe he'll be okay after this too."

Eventually, Buzz Bee started flying the right way again like nothing had happened.

"Should we tell him what happened?" the bees asked each other.

"I don't think so," said Buddy Bee. "After all, Buzz Bee is our friend and we don't want to hurt his feelings."

The bees buzzed in agreement and no one said a thing!

Can YOU find Buzz Bee?

A few weeks later, the bees were returning to the hive when Buzz Bee's friend Spike spotted something strange.

"Oh my," said Spike to the other bees, "Buzz Bee has fallen in the hive and he can't get up! This is getting serious and Buzz Bee doesn't even know these things are happening to him!"

The other bees reminded Spike what Buddy Bee had said earlier about hurting Buzz Bee's feelings by telling him how strange he was acting.

"I don't care what Buddy Bee said. I think we should tell Queenie, Buzz Bee's mommy. Someone needs to speak to Queenie about what's happening to her son, so I will!"

With that, Spike flew off to tell Buddy Bee what he was planning to do.

Buddy Bee listened carefully to Spike.

"Yes, you're right, Spike," Buddy Bee admitted. "Things seem to be getting worse. Something needs to be done and it looks like hiding what is happening to our friend isn't the answer."

Buddy Bee, Spike, and a few other bees flew away to find Queenie.

Queenie was sitting quietly when the young bees found her.

"Queenie," Spike said, "we think something is very wrong with Buzz Bee."

The bees told her all about the strange things Buzz Bee had been doing.

"And he doesn't remember doing any of it. We don't know what to do, so we thought you should know eveything that has happened," Spike said.

"Oh my!" cried Queenie. "I'm going to find my son and talk to him about all of this. Then we can figure out what to do to help him."

The bees were so happy about deciding to tell Queenie what was going on with Buzz Bee. In fact, they even agreed that they should have told her about it sooner!

Queenie went to the hive to find Buzz Bee.

"Buzz Bee," she said, "how have you been feeling lately?"

"I'm okay," he answered. "Why are you asking?"

"I've been hearing stories around the hive. Have you noticed anything different about yourself?" Queenie asked.

Buzz Bee thought for a moment.

"Yes, mommy. I have," he confessed. "The other day, I was caught in a flower and I didn't know how I got there! I was so confused," Buzz Bee said.

"Seems like quite a puzzle," Queenie said. "I think we should go visit Dr. Glowden. He's good at solving puzzles."

"What can I do for you?" asked Doctor Glowden.

Queenie told the Doctor what was happening and why she was worried about her son.

"I think I might know the problem," said the doctor. "But I would like to run three tests first."

"Wait a minute," said Buzz Bee, "will the tests hurt?"

"Oh no, not at all," the doctor answered. "In fact, most of the time you'll just lie there."

"Oh!" said Buzz Bee. "That sounds even easier than the tests I have to take at Bee school!"

So off he went to take the tests.

"Wow, what is this test? And what is THAT machine?" asked Buzz Bee.

"This test is called an E.E.G. It will show your brain waves," said Bob Bee, the test's technician.

"Waves? Like the ocean?" asked Buzz Bee.

"Yes, kind of," laughed Bob Bee.

"And what are you going to do with all of those wires?" Buzz Bee asked.

"We glue them to your head," Bob answered.

"You've got to be kidding me! I really don't think I want wires hanging from my head forever!" cried Buzz Bee.

"Don't worry, Buzz Bee," Bob reassured the young bee. "We only leave them on for the test and then they come off easily after. During the test, we'll just ask you to open and close your eyes and a few other simple things. You will be fine."

Buzz Bee nodded and they started the test. He didn't feel a bad thing the whole time and was not afraid at all by the end of it.

Test number two was a CAT scan.

"Why do they call is a CAT scan?" asked Buzz Bee, more than a little worried. "I'm not a cat. Will it turn me into one?"

"No," replied Bob Bee, "CAT is short for a big long name. You will just lie on the bed and it will move you into the machine to take pictures of the inside of your brain."

"Wait, wait! Are you really sure that won't hurt?" asked Buzz Bee.

"I didn't fool you about the last test and I won't fool you now," Bob answered.

When he found this test was as painless as the first, Buzz Bee knew he could trust Bob Bee and Doctor Glowden. However, Buzz Bee still wanted to ask a lot of questions. Thankfully, no one minded a bit!

Off to test number three! This one was called a Telemetry (te-lem-e-try).

"We will put this helmet on your head and it will measure your brain waves just like an E.E.G. Except instead of measuring them while you're just lying down, this can measure them while you are doing everyday things," explained Bob Bee.

"That E.E.G. was easy peazzy," Buzz Bee remembered. "So let's get started!"

Bob Bee put the helmet on Buzz Bee and tied a big red bow. Buzz Bee looked very cute! But he didn't look very happy.

"Wait," cried Buzz Bee, "I can't fly with this thing on my head!"

Bob Bee told him to just walk around for a few hours instead of flying around. After that, the helmet could come off and he would be able to fly just like before.

After a few hours of not flying, Bob Bee helped to remove the helmet and Buzz Bee could fly again, just like Bob had promised.

"Buzz Bee, we have great news!" said Doctor Glowden after looking at the test results. "We have found the problem and we can correct it with medicine!"

The doctor's tail was glowing brightly. It always glowed when he was happy. He explained to Buzz Bee what they had discovered from doing the tests.

"You suffer from something called seizures. There are many kinds of them. Yours are mild and they just make you feel topsy-turvy at times. That's why you've been flying into flowers. If you take medicine everyday, the seizures should go away."

Buzz Bee nodded as the doctor continued.

"Just one thing," said the doctor. "The medicine will make you feel funny for just a little while until your body gets used to it. And it will only work if you take it everyday! Do you promise you will take it?"

"Yes sir," sniffed Buzz Bee with tears in his eyes. "I'll take it everyday."

Doctor Glowden and Queenie were very happy that the cause of Buzz Bee's strange behavior was finally found, but Buzz Bee himself was not celebrating.

"I'm doomed, I'm doomed!" sobbed Buzz Bee. "I do not want to have seizures! It is so unfair! I just want to be a normal bee. I'll never fly right again!"

And Buzz Bee cried big tears.

A few days later, Buzz Bee and the other bees were flying to find nectar.

"Look," said Buzz Bee, "there are tons of flowers here! We can make lots of honey from this field!"

Buddy Bee gave Buzz Bee a strange look.

"How many flowers do you see?" he asked.

"At least fifty," answered Buzz Bee.

"I only see a few flowers," Buddy Bee said. "Maybe the medicine you've been taking is making you see funny."

Buzz Bee felt bad and Buddy Bee saw that his feelings were hurt.

"Don't feel bad, Buzz Bee. Remember how the doctor told you the medicine would make you feel this way for a little while. You'll be fine soon."

Buzz Bee felt better. Buddy Bee was his good friend and he trusted him. But he still felt strange being the only bee in the hive that had this topsy-turvy problem.

Doctor Glowden needed to see Buzz Bee again to be sure the medicine was working. In the waiting room, Buzz Bee saw two other bees.

"My name is Buzz Bee," he introduced himself. "What are your names?"

"I'm Honey and this is Billy Bee," one of the bees answered.

"Why are you two here?" asked Buzz Bee.

"We have seizures," they both answered.

"You do?" Buzz Bee asked excitedly. "I thought no one else in the whole wide world had seizures but me. Does it upset you because you're not normal?" asked Buzz Bee.

"Why do you think we aren't normal?" Honey answered. "Everyone has some problem. We are as normal as everyone else."

Buzz Bee smiled a huge smile. Honey was right. The medicine was working, he could see clearly now, he always flew straight, and he'd even found other bees like him!

"I am normal!" he realized. At last everything was very, very good.

Buzz Bee, an epileptic bee who finds out he is as normal as everyone else.

NOTES FROM YOUR DOCTOR...

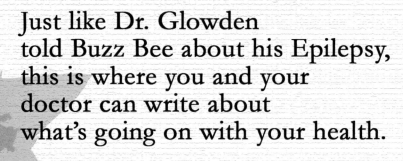

Just like Dr. Glowden
told Buzz Bee about his Epilepsy,
this is where you and your
doctor can write about
what's going on with your health.

Made in United States
Troutdale, OR
10/05/2023